MR. HAPPY's Rainy Day Activity Book

Roger Hargreaves

EGMONT
We bring stories to life

MR. MEN   LITTLE MISS

MR. MEN™ LITTLE MISS™ © THOIP (a SANRIO company)

Mr. Happy's Rainy Day Activity Book © 2016 THOIP (a SANRIO company)
Printed and published under licence from Price Stern Sloan, Inc., Los Angeles.
Published in Great Britain by Egmont UK Limited
The Yellow Building, 1 Nicholas Road, London, W11 4AN

ISBN 978 1 4052 8105 8
63222/1
Printed in China

Stay safe online. Any website addresses listed in this book are correct at the time of going to print.
However, Egmont is not responsible for content hosted by third parties. Please be aware that online content can be subject to change
and websites can contain content that is unsuitable for children. We advise that all children are supervised when using the internet.

**Parental guidance is advised for all craft and cooking activities. Always ask an adult to help when using glue,
paint, scissors, knives and other kitchen equipment. Wear protective clothing and cover surfaces to avoid staining.
Keep all small objects away from very young children, as they could present a choking hazard.**

Mr Happy in the Sunshine

Mr Happy is very happy. He lives on the other side of the world in a place called Happyland, where the sun shines hotter than here.

Finish the picture with your sunniest colours and lots of smiling faces to brighten up even the most rainy day.

Who's Who?

How well do you know Mr Happy's friends?
Can you work out who these Mr Men and Little Miss are?
Add the matching stickers and write their names if you like.

You will see more of them later as they have lots of ideas
for what to do on a rainy day!

He has arms that stretch
and stretch and stretch.
Extraordinarily long arms.

Mr _____

She is very happy, just
like Mr Happy. A ray of
sunshine on a rainy day.

Little Miss _____

He loves to eat. He is
greedy by name and
greedy by nature.

Mr _____

He is the messiest person you will ever meet in your whole life.

Mr _____

She loves to tell everyone what to do.

Little Miss _____

He has no sense at all. As you might expect, he lives in Nonsenseland.

Mr _____

She talks all the time. It's very hard to get a word in edgeways.

Little Miss _____

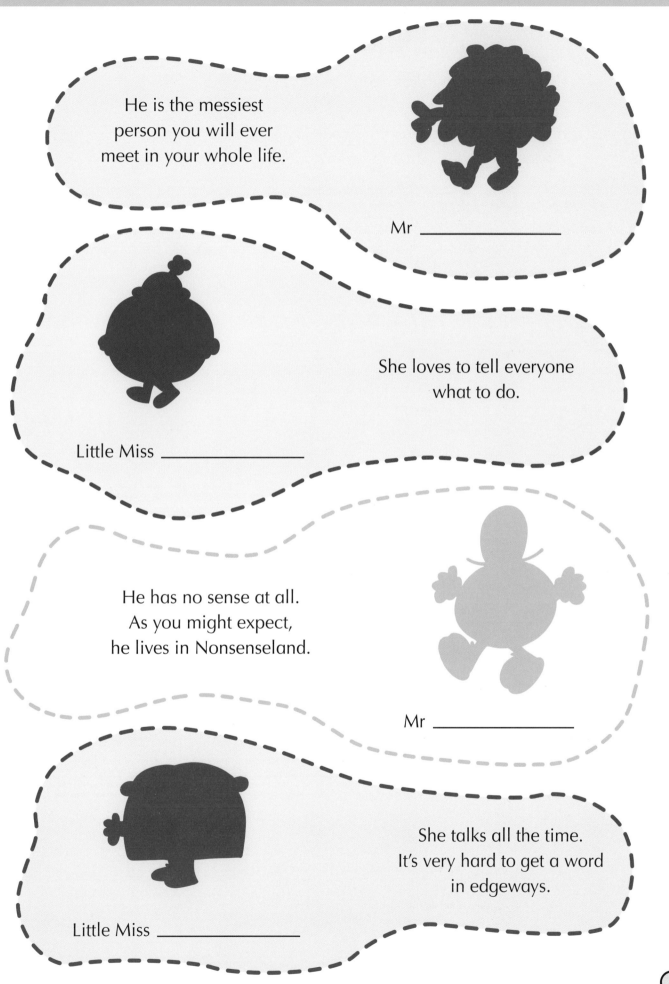

Scribbles and Shapes

Colour in the Mr Men and Little Miss before doodling some more.
Use the shapes to get you started.

Mr Nonsense's
Heads, Bodies and Legs

Here's a fun game you could play with friends.
All you need is a pen, paper and your imagination!

1. Each person gets a piece of paper and a pencil or crayon.

2. Draw a large head on your paper, with hair or a hat. Then fold it over at the top, leaving the bottom part showing. This will also be the character's body.

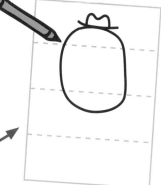

3. Now pass the paper to the person on your left. They draw a face and arms and fold the paper over again to hide the drawing.

4. The paper is passed to the left again and legs are added. You could add some funny shoes if you like!

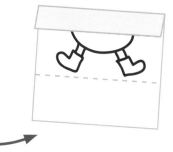

5. The papers are passed for a final time and the last person chooses a name before opening the paper to reveal a new Mr Men or Little Miss character. What will yours be called?!

Mr Fluffy

Mr Fluffy

Mr Men Paper Chain

Follow the instructions to make your own Mr Men paper chain.

You will need:

- Paper (approx. 10cm x 30cm, A4 paper cut lengthwise)
- Scissors
- Crayons and stickers
- Optional: sticky tape

Ask an adult to help .

How to make:

1. Fold the paper backwards and forwards (pleated) into four.

2. Draw a Mr Men or Little Miss on the top section of the paper. Make sure their hands touch the edge of the folded sheet.

3. Cut the character out carefully, making sure you don't cut along the folds at the ends of their hands.

4. Unfold the paper to reveal a chain of Mr Men or Little Miss holding hands.

5. You can now draw their face and colour them in with your brightest colours.

To have more Mr Men or Little Miss in your chain, use a larger sheet of paper and fold more pleats before cutting. Alternatively, use more than one sheet of paper and connect the Mr Men or Little Miss with sticky tape.

Mr Men Matching

The Mr Men are seeing double!
Can you find the character who doesn't have a twin?

Add the matching sticker here.

How to Draw Little Miss Sunshine

Step 1

Get started by ...
Drawing a round body with little arms and legs.

Step 2

Next ...

Add two oval shapes with lines for her hair. Then she needs her eyes and nose and a big smile!

Step 3

Don't forget...
Those plaits, the little bows and her cute freckles!

Step 4

Finally …

Find your sunniest yellow crayon to colour her in. And a cheery red crayon for her ribbons.

Draw your own Little Miss Sunshine here.

Little Miss Doodle

Doodle some hair, hats and accessories on these Little Miss!

Little Miss Splendid

Little Miss Chatterbox

Little Miss Giggles

Little Miss Sunshine

Splendid Scribbles

Little Miss Splendid has a splendid idea for a drawing game you can play with friends. Just make sure she looks suitably splendid if you choose her!

You will need:

- Paper
- Pencils
- Mr Men character cards – These can be found at the back of the book. Simply cut along the dashed lines and they're ready to use!
- Optional: timer or stopwatch

How to play:

1. Put the Mr Men cards face down on the table.

2. The first player picks a card and looks at which Mr Men they have, making sure no one else can see it.

3. Now it's time to draw your Mr Men character and see who can guess first! You can set a timer or stopwatch to 60 seconds and do it against the clock if you like.

4. Whoever guesses correctly is the next person to draw. If no one guesses, you can have another turn. You can also take it in turns to draw to give your hands a rest!

Messy Making

Mr Messy is the messiest person you'll ever meet in your whole life.
Follow the instructions to make your very own Mr Messy out of tissue paper!

You will need:

- Pink coloured tissue paper
- A sheet of white paper
- Glue
- Black felt tip pen

Method:

1. Tear up the tissue paper into small pieces.

2. Scrunch up the pieces into small balls.

3. Stick the balls of tissue paper onto the paper to create your Mr Messy.

4. Give Mr Messy two eyes and a big smile.

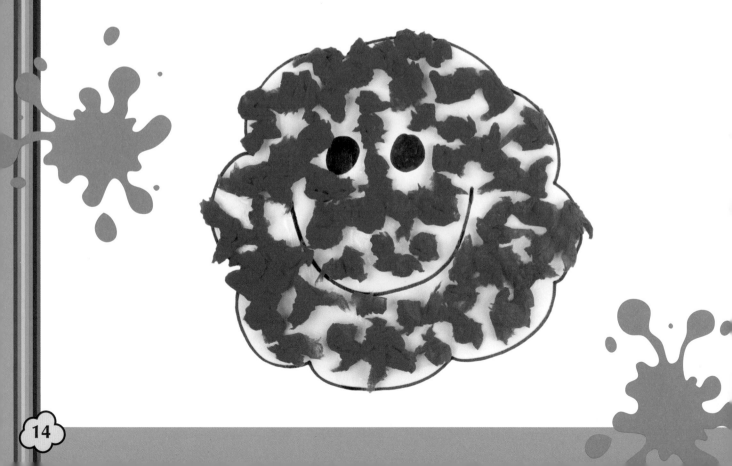

And if that isn't messy enough, try painting Mr Messy with a ball !

Ball

Tray

You will need:

- A tray
- A sheet of white paper
- A bowl of pink paint
- A small ball
- Scissors
- Black felt tip pen

Piece of paper

Bowl of pink paint

Method:

1. Place your paper on the tray.

2. Dip the ball in the paint.

3. Drop the ball on the tray and roll it around.

4. When your picture is dry, cut it out in the shape of Mr Messy and draw on his happy face!

Eggstraordinary Mr Men Eggs

Mr Strong loves eggs. The more eggs he eats, the stronger he becomes. Follow these easy steps to create your own eggstraordinary Mr Men eggs!

You will need:

- Boiled Eggs
- Card
- Paint
- Felt tips
- Scissors
- Glue

Ask an adult to help .

Method:

1. Choose which Mr Men characters you would like to create and paint your eggs in the matching colours. You can stand your eggs on a small piece of card, like a toilet roll tube, to make painting easier.

2. Now draw their arms on the card and paint them to match your Mr Men. Remember to add a little extra to your arms as a flap, so that you can glue them onto your eggs. When the paint is dry, cut out your arms.
You could use a longer piece of folded card for Mr Tickle's arms and you could make a blue hat out of card!

3. When your eggs are dry, glue on the arms with the tabs.

4. Then use your felt tip pens to draw their faces.

Your eggstraordinary eggs are ready!

Mr Strong Keep Out – these eggs are NOT to be eaten!

Cooking Counting

These eggs **are** to be eaten! It's fun to make and bake things on a rainy day.
Count the food below and then write the totals in the boxes.

Kitchen Kit

Mr Happy and his friends are about to do some cooking.
Can you circle the object that doesn't belong in the kitchen?

Mr Men Restaurant

Would you like to create your own Mr Men restaurant at home?
Just follow this handy guide!

1. Choose a name for your restaurant. Be as creative as you like. How about **Mr Tickle's Tasty Treats** or **Little Miss Dotty's Diner?**

2. Pick a place and decorate the space. Will your restaurant have a table and chairs or cushions and a blanket? Will it be as colourful as Mr Funny?!

3. Decide which role you will play. Are you going to be the chef, a waiter or a customer? You might need Mr Strong to carry all those cakes!

4. Draw up your menu. What delicious dishes will be on it? How about **Mr Greedy's Giant Burger, Mr Happy's Sunny Salad** and **Little Miss Sunshine's Strawberry Surprise?**

5. Get busy in the kitchen. Have fun pretending to cook with play food or ask an adult to help you make some real meals to eat. Be careful, Mr Bump!

6. Time to serve your customers. Get ready to take those orders and dish up your tasty treats. Don't forget to ask your customers to pay – Mr Mean won't allow a restaurant that serves free food!

Mr Perfect's Pizza

Mr Perfect has the perfect idea for how to make his friends smile. Follow these instructions to make your own Mr Men pizza.

Method:

1. Use a pre-prepared pizza base.

2. Spread tomato sauce and sprinkle cheese over the base.

3. Black olives or cherry tomatoes make great eyes.

4. A strip of pepper makes a nice smile.

5. A mushroom or pepperoni slice is a good nose.

6. You could use ham or sweetcorn for hair!

7. Ask an adult to put your Mr Men pizza in a medium oven until the ingredients are hot and properly cooked.

8. Enjoy!

> Ask an adult to help you when using a sharp knife.

Why not have fun making your breakfast, lunch and pudding into a Mr Men face? Who will you choose?

Cooking Chaos

Can you spot 8 differences between these two pictures of Mr Bump, Mr Noisy and Mr Funny in the kitchen? Colour in a cake as you spot each one.

Mr Greedy's Fruit Smoothie

Mr Greedy is hungry! Follow this recipe to make a delicious fruit smoothie.

Ingredients:

- 225g strawberries (stems removed)
- One banana (sliced)
- 300ml cold milk
- 3 tablespoons of natural yogurt
- Extra strawberries, to serve (optional)

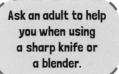

Method:

1. Tip the strawberries and banana into a food processor with the milk and yogurt.

2. Blend until your drink is smooth and creamy.

3. Pour into tall glasses and top with sliced strawberries.

4. Enjoy!

Ask an adult to help you when using a sharp knife or a blender.

Mr Silly's Spaghetti Challenge

Have you ever built a burger or a club sandwich? Mr Silly challenges you to use marshmallows to join lengths of spaghetti together to make a tower! What do you need to do to make a tall structure that remains standing?

You will need:

- Packet of spaghetti (uncooked)
- Packet of marshmallows

This tower is NOT to be eaten!

Top tip: Start by pushing the spaghetti into the marshmallow to make a cube or a pyramid.

Mr Jelly's Wobbly Jelly

Follow the instructions to make a tasty jelly you can eat!

Ingredients:

- 600ml fruit juice (any flavour you like)
- 4 gelatine leaves
- 1 handful fruit (optional)

Method:

1. Soak the gelatine leaves in a few tablespoons of juice.

2. Ask an adult to heat the rest of the juice in a pan until hot, but not boiling.

Ask an adult to help you when using a sharp knife or very hot water.

3. They can then add the softened gelatine leaves one by one and the dissolving juice. Stir until dissolved.

4. Leave to cool then pour into individual bowls or a jelly mould.

5. You can add fresh or tinned fruit if you like.

6. Put your jelly in the fridge to set. This will take about 4 hours.

7. When your jelly is wobbly, eat and enjoy!

Mr Men Biscuits

Make Mr Happy smile with these delicious biscuits!
Ask an adult to help you when using a hot oven.

Ingredients:

- 100g/3½oz unsalted butter, softened at room temperature
- 100g/3½oz caster sugar
- 1 free-range egg, lightly beaten
- 275g/10oz plain flour
- 1 tsp vanilla extract

To decorate:

- 400g/14oz icing sugar
- 3-4 tbsp water
- 2-3 drops of food colouring
- Icing pens and sweets

Ask an adult to help .

Method:

1. Preheat the oven to 190C/375F/Gas 5. Line a baking tray with greaseproof paper.

2. Beat the butter and sugar together in a bowl until combined.

3. Beat in the egg and vanilla extract, a little at a time, until well combined.

4. Stir in the flour until the mixture comes together as a dough.

5. Roll the dough out on a lightly floured work surface to a thickness of 1cm/½in.

6. Using round and square biscuit cutters, cut biscuits out of the dough and carefully place onto the baking tray.

7. Bake the biscuits for 8-10 minutes, or until golden-brown. Set aside to harden for 5 minutes, then cool on a wire rack.

8. For the icing, sift the icing sugar into a large mixing bowl and stir in enough water to create a smooth mixture. Stir in the food colouring.

9. Carefully spread the icing onto the biscuits using a knife and set aside until the icing hardens.

10. You can now draw faces with icing pens or use sweets to add character!

Little Miss Scatterbrain Potato Painting

Little Miss Scatterbrain would like to paint a picture, but she's ended up in the kitchen with the vegetables! Though she's not got it completely wrong as you can paint pictures with potatoes - just follow these instructions!

You will need:

- Potatoes
- Knife
- Chopping board
- Paint
- Paper plates
- Paper

Method:

1. Wash and towel dry the potatoes.

2. Ask an adult to cut a potato in half. They can carve out shapes at the bottom or carve the entire section into a shape.

3. Make wedges or keep the trimmings for stamping smaller shapes and details.

> Ask an adult to help you when using a sharp knife.

4. Once you have made enough potato stamps, prepare different colours of paint on the paper plates.

5. Dip a potato stamp in paint, making sure that the bottom is evenly-coated in paint.

6. Stamp your potato shapes to make your Mr Men characters. Use the wedges and trimmings to add arms, legs and faces.

7. For added fun, use your fingers to paint details on your pictures!

Little Miss Bossy Says ...

"Everybody sit in the middle of the floor! We are about to play Little Miss Bossy Says! Nobody does anything unless Little Miss Bossy (that's you or one of your friends) says so, and if Little Miss Bossy says so, you must do it! If you get it wrong, you must leave the floor. Are we all clear on that? Okay! We'll start now. The winner is the last person left."

 Little Miss Bossy says pull a funny face like Mr Funny

Bounce like Mr Bounce (if you did this, you're out!)

 Little Miss Bossy says giggle like Little Miss Giggles

Little Miss Bossy says shout your name as loud as Mr Noisy

Little Miss Bossy says wobble like Mr Jelly

Little Miss Bossy says reach for the sky like Mr Tall

 Tickle your tummy like Mr Tickle (if you did this, you're out!)

Little Miss Bossy says flex your muscles like Mr Strong

 Clap your hands for Little Miss Star (if you did this, you're out!)

Little Miss Bossy says hug like Little Miss Hug

You can have fun making up your own Mr Men style actions too!

Mr Muddle's Maze

It's raining heavily and Mr Muddle has got in a muddle again and can't find his way home. Can you help him, avoiding the big puddles on the way?

28

My Mr Men House

The Mr Men have some splendidly silly and muddled houses.
Mr Funny lives in a teapot and Mr Nonsense's house is in a tree.

Create your own Mr Men-style house.

Mr Men Road Trip

Mr Funny and his friends are going on a camping trip.

Can you find:

- A tennis racket
- Mr Nonsense
- A red hat
- A flower
- A cake

Indoor Camp

Mr Nonsense likes to go camping, in his house, up a tree. Have you ever built your own indoor camp? If it's raining outside, you can just bring the fun indoors! Here are some handy tips:

1. Gather your camping gear.

Pack a rucksack with all those camping-trip essentials: snacks, drinks, a torch, books and games. Create your own personal survival kit. Mr Greedy likes to bring forty sandwiches!

2. Choose a pitch.

A quiet corner where you can have some space and privacy is perfect. Mr Quiet always knows the perfect spot.

3. Build a den.

A table and chairs make a great framework. Just drape them with sheets or throws. A long-handled broom can be used to prop up the cover and add some height to the doorway. Mr Silly likes to use spaghetti!

Keep Out!

4. Get comfortable.

Pile in pillows and blankets to get comfortable. Try not to sleep the whole time like Mr Lazy.

5. Make a 'Keep Out' sign.

Using a piece of card, a length of string and some paint, make your own 'Keep Out' sign to remind the grown-ups that this is a parent-free zone. Now you can relax and play in your own private hideaway. Mr Nosey is NOT allowed!

For even more fun, you could make some Mr Men shapes out of cardboard and use your torch to create a shadow story on the side of your tent!

Happy Campers

Finish this picture of Little Miss Sunshine and her friends camping in the countryside. You could add some stickers too.

Have you ever had an indoor picnic? Just lay down your picnic blanket and get out your favourite snacks to bring some sunshine indoors.

Confused Campers

Mr Bump and Mr Funny are very late for the camping trip.
Who will follow the right path to reach the tent before bedtime?

Answer: Mr Funny

Mr Men Minefield

Can you use your Mr Men books or character cards to get across your
bedroom without standing on the floor?

Ask a friend to create a path across your room with the books or cards.
The path can all be on the floor or it can go over your bed, chair or table.
If you touch the floor, Mr Tickle will come and tickle you!

Make your own Treasure Map

Follow the instructions to make your very own treasure map.

You will need:

- White paper
- Teabags
- Small bowl of cold water
- Felt tip pens
- String or ribbon

Method:

1. Take your piece of white paper and rip the edges a bit.

2. Dip the teabag into the water and wipe it over both sides of the white paper.

3. Let the paper dry, then use your pens to draw on your map. There should be a dotted trail that winds around the map to an X. You could create a trail around the rooms in your house!

4. Once you've drawn the trail and the X, you can label some obstacles, like Mr Bump's Bridge, Mr Tall's Tower and Mr Mischief's Mountain.

5. Roll your map up into a scroll and use your string or ribbon to tie a bow around it.

Treasure Hunt

Now you've made your treasure map, why not go on a treasure hunt?! Will you be Little Miss Lucky and find all the treasure or Mr Muddle and get lost following the map? Don't worry Mr Jelly, there are no pirates!

You will need:

- Your treasure map
- Some treasure (whatever you like, it could be spare change or a Mr Men book!)
- Optional: costumes and clues

Method:

1. You don't need a theme to do a treasure hunt, but pretending to be someone else is lots of fun. This is a Mr Men treasure hunt, so you can be your favourite character if you like.

2. It's more exciting to follow clues, so ask an adult if they can write some clues for you. Here are a few ideas:

> **Clue 1: Mr Greedy is in a hungry mood, follow him here to find some food.** (Clue 2 will be in the kitchen)
>
> **Clue 2: Add some colour to your day, pick these up and you're on your way.** (Clue 3 will be with the colouring pencils)
>
> **Clue 3: Take a look in a favourite book.** (Clue 4 will be in a Mr Men book)

3. Hide your treasure and your clues if you're using them. Make sure they match the treasure map you're following!

4. The hunt begins! Remember to work as a team, and if you need help, you can ask the hider to say hotter or colder so you know how close you are. Cheer, clap and celebrate as loudly as Mr Noisy when you find the treasure!

Mr Small's Hunt the Thimble

Mr Small is very small, as small as a thimble. This game is almost like playing hide and seek with Mr Small. Remember to be as nosey as Mr Nosey, so you can find the thimble!

You will need:

A thimble (or other small object, such as a button, coin or toy. You can also use one of your Mr Men books)

How to play:

1. One person is chosen to hide the thimble.

2. Everyone else leaves the room while the thimble is hidden. You must be able to see the thimble - so no moving the furniture or hiding it in drawers or cupboards, but you can cleverly hide it against something of a similar colour or shape to make it harder to find!

3. When the thimble is hidden, everyone is called back in and the race begins to be the first to find it. You can say hotter or colder depending on how close people are to the thimble if you like!

4. The winner is the next person to hide the thimble, and the game continues.

Lost Letters

Oh no, the letters are missing from the names of these Mr Men.
They will not be happy! Can you fill in the missing letters to complete
the names of these Mr Men.

M_ Fu_sy

Mr G_um_y

Li_tle Mi_s B_ssy

Small Sudoku

Use your Mr Small, Little Miss Tiny, Mr Bounce and Mr Quiet stickers
to finish this small sudoku.

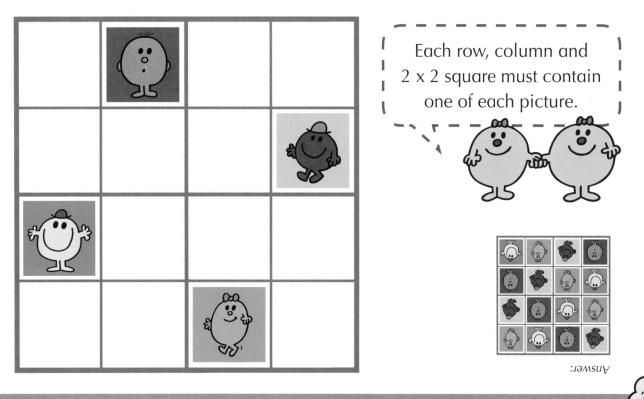

Each row, column and
2 x 2 square must contain
one of each picture.

Who am I?

How well do you know the Mr Men? Would you be able to guess which Mr Men character you are with a few simple questions? Now is your chance to find out!

You will need:

Mr Men character cards and sticky tape OR sticky notes and pencils

How to play:

1. Choose one of the Mr Men character cards and tape it to your friend's back, making sure they don't see it. Or you can write the name of a Mr Men character on a sticky note instead if you like.

2. Your friend will do the same for you.

3. You now take it in turns to ask 'yes or no' questions to work out who you are. For example, "Am I male?", "Do I wear a hat?", "Am I red?"

4. When you think you know who you are, simply make your guess and the first person to guess correctly wins the game!

Spot and Say

How good are you at finding people in a crowd? See if you can spot the Mr Men and Little Miss meeting these descriptions! Who else is hiding in the crowd?

Wearing glasses ☐

With a moustache ☐

Wearing a crown ☐

There are two of them ☐

With a red nose ☐

With orange, curly hair ☐

Wearing odd shoes ☐

Wearing a spotty hat ☐

Very tall ☐

Very small ☐

Answer: Walter the worm

Ready to Rush?

Are you ready for Mr Rush's scavenger hunt?
On your marks, get set, rush!

You will need:

- Scavenger hunt list
- Pens or pencils
- A bag to collect your things (If you use a paper bag, you can write the list on it)

How to play:

1. Create a list of objects or use this list. You can get creative with things to find in different colours, shapes and sizes.

Mr Men List

- Toothbrush for Mr Tickle
- An apple for Mr Greedy
- Something yellow for Mr Happy
- A tissue for Mr Sneeze
- A plaster for Mr Bump
- Two of something for Little Miss Twins
- A ruler for Little Miss Neat
- A hat for Little Miss Splendid
- A hairbrush for Little Miss Sunshine
- A book for Little Miss Curious

2. Run around the house collecting all the things on the list. You can tick them off your list as you go.

3. The first one back with all the things is the winner OR after 5 minutes each player must return to the kitchen where an adult counts who has the most items from the list.

Mr Bounce's Ball Game

Mr Bounce is very small, and bounces all over the place like a rubber ball. Here is a fun, bouncing game you can play with balls. You have to hop on one leg while you play, so you're as bouncy as Mr Bounce!

You will need:

- 2 boules each. These can be any kind of balls!
- A jack. You could use one of your Mr Men books or toys.

How to play:

1. Choose a throw line where you will stand to throw your boules. You could create one with your books.

2. Now choose who will throw the jack.

3. Each person takes it in turns to throw a boule towards the jack.

4. Then everyone takes it in turn to throw the second boule.

5. The boule that finishes closest to the jack wins!

DID YOU KNOW?
Boules is a type of ball game popular in France. The aim is to throw your ball, or *'boule'*, closest to the target, which is called a *'jack'*.

Mr Bounce is also very good at bouncing on the bed!

Holiday Dreams

Little Miss Chatterbox is dreaming she is on a beach in the sunshine! Study the picture for one minute then cover it up and see how much you can remember.

1. Who is playing volleyball with Mr Happy? ....

2. What is Mr Bump wearing? ....

3. What colour is the lilo? ....

4. How many clouds are there? ....

5. Who is paragliding? ....

Mr Clever has a fun memory game you can play. All you need is a tray, some small objects and a tea towel. You've got a minute to memorise what is on the tray! How many will you remember?

42

Little Miss Chatterbox Whispers

Little Miss Chatterbox talks all the time. She even talks in her sleep. This game works well if there are lots of you! But you must remember to be as quiet as Mr Quiet!

How to play:

1. Everyone sits in a circle.

2. One person chooses a message to whisper into the ear of the person next to them. The message can be serious or very silly! You can write down the message in case anyone is a Mr Forgetful.

3. The next person now whispers the message to the person next to them, and so on around the circle.

4. When the message has been whispered to the last person, they have to say aloud what they think was whispered to them.

5. The first person then reveals the real message. Celebrate if the messages match and giggle if they don't!

You can write your funniest whispers here!

How to Draw Mr Tickle

Step 1

Get started by ...
Drawing a simple round body.

Step 2

Next ...
Add feet, a big smile
and eyes.

Step 3

And then ...
Colour him in orange and
add his little blue hat.
And he's finished.

Draw your own Mr Tickle here. Then keep your eyes wide open for an unsuspecting someone to tickle!

Modelling Dough Recipe

Follow the instructions to make lots of your own dough
in any colour you like.

You will need:

- 2 cups of plain flour
- 1 cup of salt
- 2 tablespoons of cream of tartar
- 2 tablespoons of oil
- 2 cups of water
- 1 teaspoon of food colouring

Ask an adult to help .

Method:

1. Mix all the ingredients in a saucepan.

2. Ask an adult to stir the mixture over a low heat until it goes lumpy. Keep stirring and it will go smooth and form a dough.

3. Remember to let it cool before playing!

4. Keep it in an airtight container when you are not using it so it doesn't dry out.

**Mr Greedy Keep Out - this recipe is
definitely NOT to be eaten!**

Mr Men Modelling

Now you have your own dough to make whichever Mr Men you like!
Who will you create? Here are some fun ideas:

Mr Tickle

Mr Dizzy

**You can even play a fun guessing game with your modelling dough.
The only difference is that you have to make your Mr Men character,
instead of drawing it!**

Mr Men Board Game

Here's a fun game for you to play with a friend. It's the day of Mr Happy's party and storm clouds are rumbling overhead. Who will get to his house first?

START

Ask a friend to play with you. Then find a dice and two counters (you could use coins for counters). The first person to roll a six starts the game, and the winner is the first person to reach Mr Happy's house home and dry!

1

2

Mr Tickle tries to tickle you. Go forward one space.

3

4

Mr Muddle sends you the wrong way. Go back one space.

7

Little Miss Chatterbox stops you for a chat. Go back one space.

5

6

8

A Bit of a Blur

Can you work out who's who from these blurred pictures?
Shout out their names or you can write them on the lines if you like.

Little Miss

Little Miss

Little Miss

. . . .

. . . .

. . . .

Which Mr Men?

Can you crack the clues to work out which Mr Men is being
described? The sooner you get it, the better your Mr Men knowledge.
Add the matching sticker and write his name when you've got it.

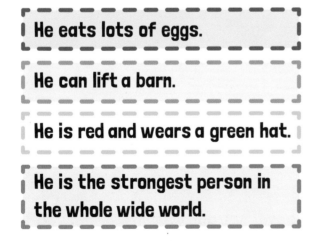

> He eats lots of eggs.

> He can lift a barn.

> He is red and wears a green hat.

> He is the strongest person in
> the whole wide world.

Mr . . . .

Little Miss Star's Charades

Little Miss Star has a fun game for all budding stars. All you need is your Mr Men character cards and your best acting skills!

How to play:

1. Put your Mr Men character cards in a pile face-down and look at the top card, making sure your friend can't see it.

2. Now act out the character to your friends. Any actions or noises are allowed, but NO words!

3. Your friends have to guess which character you are and the first person to guess correctly goes next.

4. You can also take it in turns to act or if no one guesses, you can have another turn.

MR. NOI

MR. FUNN

LITTLE MISS SHY

If you like pretending to be a Mr Men or Little Miss, why not act out one of the stories or make up your own? You could get out your dress-up clothes and put on your own play with a stage and seats for the audience!

Mr Men Dress Up

Here are some fun ideas for how to dress up as one of the Mr Men.

Mr Tickle

Mr Tickle has extraordinarily long arms. To make Mr Tickle's extraordinarily long arms, stuff orange-coloured long tights, then fasten them to an orange t-shirt and tie onto your arms.

Mr Happy

Mr Happy is very happy. Dress in yellow and draw a big smile on your t-shirt or you could make a tabard out of a large piece of cardboard and draw on a happy face!

Mr Bump

Mr Bump is the sort of person who is always having accidents. Dress in blue and wrap lots of bandages (or loo roll!) around yourself.

Mr Greedy

Mr Greedy loves to eat. Dress up all in pink and put a big cushion up your top to create his distinctive tummy! Make sure you have lots of food with you!

Mr Messy

Mr Messy is the messiest person you will ever meet in your whole life. Dress up all in pink, but this time, make sure you look really messy!

Mr Topsy-Turvy

Everything about Mr Topsy-Turvy is either inside out, back to front, topsy-turvy in fact. Turn your clothes inside out or back to front and then do everything opposite.

Make Mr Uppity's Hat

Follow the instructions to make your own top hat like Mr Uppity.

You will need:

- Two sheets of black card
- Pencil
- Scissors
- Sticky tape

Ask an adult to help.

How to make:

1. Roll a piece of black card to fit around your head. Then tape the ends together.

2. Draw around the inside of your roll of card to create a circle on your other sheet of card.

3. Now using a large bowl or plate as a guide, draw another circle to create the brim of Mr Uppity's hat.

4. Cut around the brim of the hat and then cut out the hole for your head – you will need this circle later.

5. Tape the roll of black card to the brim, then stick the other circle on the top.

Your Mr Uppity's hat is ready!

The Mr Men Game

Is being indoors making you sleepy? Have fun running around pretending to be different Mr Men! When someone says the name of a character you have to move like him. Here are some ideas:

Mr Rush
move fast

Mr Slow
move slowly

Mr Jelly
shake your whole body

Mr Muddle
walk backwards

Mr Tall
stretch up and move

Mr Small
crouch and move

Mr Strong
move flexing your muscles

Mr Bounce
bounce!

Why not come up with your own ideas – and don't forget the Little Miss characters or Little Miss Bossy will be very unhappy!

Little Miss Somersault's Challenge

Now you've warmed up, are you ready for Little Miss Somersault's indoor obstacle course? All you need is some obstacles and lots of energy!

Here are some ideas:

1. Bunny hop (hop forward with feet together) five times.

2. Crawl through a tunnel. You can create a tunnel by lining up some chairs and placing a sheet over them.

3. Walk over several pillows or sofa cushions that are on the floor with spaces in between them.

4. Climb over a footstool or pile of books.

5. Use a large cooking spoon to transfer five blocks or other small toys one at a time into a container placed several feel away.

6. Do five jumping jacks.

7. Side-step five times.

8. Toss five soft balls or soft toys into a laundry basket several feet away.

9. "Walk the tightrope!" Place a skipping rope or tape measure on the floor and walk across it, heel to toe.

10. Bunny hop five more times to the finish line!

Use your imagination to come up with your own fun ideas. You could ask an adult to help you set up the obstacle course. You may need to ask them to shout out instructions, so you know what to do at each obstacle. You could even ask them to time you and award medals at the end of the course!

Make Some Noise

Mr Noisy is a very noisy person indeed.
Follow these instructions to make a very noisy maraca!

You will need:

- Water bottle
- Masking tape
- Paint
- Paintbrush
- Marker pens
- Paper for funnel
- Uncooked rice

How to make:

1. Wrap an empty, travel-size water bottle with masking tape, leaving the cap free.

2. Decorate the bottle using paint or markers and let it dry.

3. Put two handfuls of uncooked rice into the bottle. A paper funnel makes it easier.

4. Replace the cap tightly, then shake, shake, shake to make some noise!

Why not start a band? Use tissue boxes and elastic bands to make a guitar, paper plates with milk bottle tops to make a tambourine and bang pans with wooden spoons for drums. Get ready to shake, rattle and roll!

Have a Dance Party

Little Miss Fun loves parties and what better time to have a party than a rainy day! Pull out those hairbrush microphones and play your favourite songs for a fun dance party!

Take it in turns to play DJ for a few songs and dance the rain away. You could even give prizes for the most inventive Mr Men dance move!

Listen to the sounds of rain

When you feel in a need of a rest, why not spend a few minutes just listening to the sounds of the rain. Set out various objects (like metal, plastic and glass containers) to see how water droplets sound when they hit different surfaces.

Sing in the Rain!

If being indoors has left you feeling like you've got ants in your pants, then get on your rain gear and go outside! Sing in the rain and have fun puddle splashing! Then afterwards, have a warm bath and snuggle up in your PJs.

Go on a safari

Wet weather brings out creatures you might not normally see, like worms and snails. It's also fun to go searching for animals that are trying to seek shelter from the rain, like birds and spiders.

Become a scientist

Stand on the pavement with an adult and watch the water flow by in the gutter. Where is the water going and how fast is it moving? Sticks, small pieces of wood and leaves all make great boats. Which items make the fastest boats? Which sail the furthest?

Make some rain art

Use paper plates, some food colouring and rain droplets to make rain art. Mr Messy also loves mud painting!

Don't forget to collect some leaves, stones, sticks and other natural items while you're outside.

Rainy Day Crafts

Now you're warm and dry inside, why not use some of the things you collected from outside to create some fun Mr Men pictures?

Here are some ideas:

Stick a real flower to a picture of Little Miss Bossy

Decorate some stones with your favourite Mr Men!

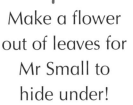

Make a flower out of leaves for Mr Small to hide under!

Follow these instructions to make a sailboat for your next trip into the rain.

1. Begin with a square piece of paper, any size.

2. To make a square, fold paper diagonally and cut off the excess paper.

3. To make the boat, begin by folding one of the folded points inward toward the other side at a slight angle. The tip of the point you are folding will be the top of the boat.

4. Open the square back up and do a 'reverse' fold to create the sides of the boat. Your ship is set to sail!

You could also get creative with cardboard. Why not make Mr Silly's car with square wheels or a Nonsenseland house out of a cardboard box?!

? Curious Questions ?

Little Miss Curious is very curious. There are two things she would like to know.

Who is your favourite Mr Men or Little Miss character?

What is your favourite rainy day activity?

**Doodle a drawing, write about them or
stick your pictures here!**

MR. TICKLE

MR. GREEDY

MR. HAPPY

MR. BUMP

MR. MESSY

MR. SMALL

MR. NOISY

MR. FUNNY

MR. STRONG

LITTLE MISS
BOSSY

LITTLE MISS
NAUGHTY

LITTLE MISS
SUNSHINE

LITTLE MISS
GIGGLES

LITTLE MISS
SHY

LITTLE MISS
SPLENDID

LITTLE MISS
CHATTERBOX

LITTLE MISS
SCATTERBRAIN

LITTLE MISS
FUN

Cut along dotted lines